ABOUT THE BANK STREET READY-TO-READ SERIES

More than seventy-five years of educational research, innovative teaching, and quality publishing have earned The Bank Street College of Education its reputation as America's most trusted name in early childhood education.

Because no two children are exactly alike in their development, the Bank Street Ready-to-Read series is written on three levels to accommodate the individual stages of reading readiness of children ages three through eight.

○ *Level 1:* **GETTING READY TO READ (Pre-K–Grade 1)**
Level 1 books are perfect for reading aloud with children who are getting ready to read or just starting to read words or phrases. These books feature large type, repetition, and simple sentences.

● *Level 2:* **READING TOGETHER (Grades 1–3)**
These books have slightly smaller type and longer sentences. They are ideal for children beginning to read by themselves who may need help.

○ *Level 3:* **I CAN READ IT MYSELF (Grades 2–3)**
These stories are just right for children who can read independently. They offer more complex and challenging stories and sentences.

All three levels of The Bank Street Ready-to-Read books make it easy to select the books most appropriate for your child's development and enable him or her to grow with the series step by step. The levels purposely overlap to reinforce skills and further encourage reading.

We feel that making reading fun is the single most important thing anyone can do to help children become good readers. We hope you will become part of Bank Street's long tradition of learning through sharing.

The Bank Street College of Education

To Jonathan Matthew Davies
— W.H.H.

For a free color catalog describing Gareth Stevens' list of high-quality books and multimedia programs, call 1-800-542-2595 (USA) or 1-800-461-9120 (Canada). Gareth Stevens Publishing's Fax: (414) 225-0377. See our catalog, too, on the World Wide Web: http://gsinc.com

Library of Congress Cataloging-in-Publication Data

Hooks, William H.
    Mr. Garbage / by William H. Hooks; illustrated by Kate Duke.
      p. cm. -- (Bank Street ready-to-read)
      Summary: Five-year-old Eli's enthusiasm for saving the planet gets out of hand as he continues to fill his room with more and more junk he intends to recycle.
    ISBN 0-8368-1756-7 (lib. bdg.)
    [1. Recycling (Waste)--Fiction. 2. Environmental protection--Fiction.]
    I. Duke, Kate, ill. II. Title. III. Series.
    PZ7.H7664Msf 1997
    [E]--dc21   97-1626

This edition first published in 1997 by
Gareth Stevens Publishing
1555 North RiverCenter Drive, Suite 201
Milwaukee, Wisconsin 53212 USA

Printed in Mexico

1 2 3 4 5 6 7 8 9 01 00 99 98 97

Mr. Garbage

by William H. Hooks
Illustrated by Kate Duke

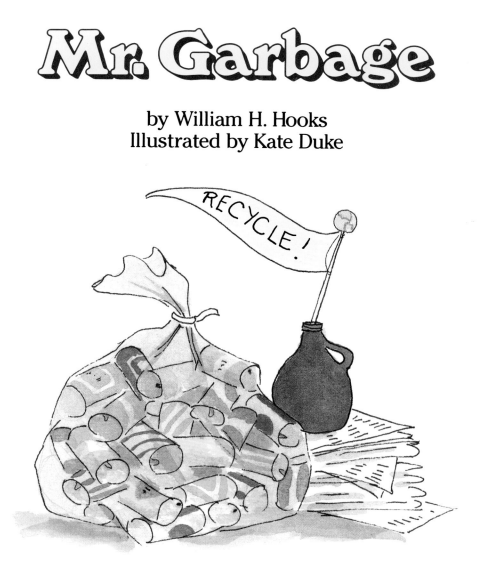

RECYCLE!

A Byron Preiss Book

Gareth Stevens Publishing
MILWAUKEE

LOWER MILLS

Earth Day

It was Earth Day in the park when my
brother, Eli, got started on his new kick.
My friend Roberta and I were going.
Mom asked us to take Eli along.
Other kids Eli's age were playing
on the swings and monkey bars.

But not Eli.
He pushed right up to the speaker's stand
where a man was talking about recycling.
"Our planet is sinking under mountains
of garbage," said the man.
"But garbage can be great stuff—
if you recycle!"

He had big plastic bags full of cans.
"See these cans?
Enough here to make a new bicycle!
You, too, can help save the world!
Recycle!"

The man pointed to a stack of magazines.
"Enough here to save a tree!" he shouted.
"You, too, can save the earth.
Recycle is the key.
Let me hear you say
the magic word, *recycle*!"

The crowd roared, "RECYCLE! RECYCLE!"
Eli was spellbound.
He kept on shouting, "Recycle!"
after the rest of the crowd had stopped.

Roberta and I dragged Eli away
for free ice cream and popcorn.

But he kept on chanting,
"Garbage is great stuff!
Recycle! Recycle!"

Now Eli tells everyone,
"I'm going to save our planet."
Grown-ups think that's pretty funny
coming from a five-year-old kid.
But they don't know Eli.

EARTH
by Eli

They smile at him and ask, "How?"
Eli is smart, I have to admit.
So he answers a question with a question.
"Do you know our planet is sinking
in a big pile of garbage?"
They think it's a joke.
But I know it's not.

Right now it's the room Eli and I share
that's sinking under a big pile of garbage.

Newspapers, magazines, soda cans, bottles,
and plastic junk are all over the room.
It's so bad I've started calling him
Mr. Garbage.

DISASTER!

From one newspaper and two soda cans,
our room has grown into a garbage dump.
Mr. Garbage has piles of newspapers
all the way to the ceiling.
The place is knee deep in cans
and bottles and junk.
I told Mom, "We're a disaster
just waiting to happen."

"Try to put up with it," Mom said.
"Eli's class is recycling
to raise money for a class trip."

18

I moaned and said, "Mom, in another week Mr. Garbage will have us both buried. This is getting dangerous!"

Just then Mr. Garbage walked in.
I mean he staggered in
with his arms full of trash.
"Look at all this great stuff!"
he said, very pleased with himself.
Mom winked at me and whispered,
"It will all be gone soon."

I groaned and went outside
to slam some balls around.

I was still pretty ticked off
by the time we went to bed.
Eli could tell I was upset.
Just as I was settling in,
he asked in a sad little voice,
"Jon, would you read me this book?"

He climbed up on a pile of newspapers
and pushed the book up to my bunk.
I looked at the title:
100 Ways Kids Can Save Our Planet.

"No way, Mr. Garbage," I told him.
"If you learn one more way,
someone is going to have to come
and save your big brother."

I don't think he got it.
But he climbed back into his bunk
and we both went to sleep.

Sometime during the night I woke up
dry as a piece of toast.
"Must have been those fish sticks
I had for supper," I thought.
I climbed down from my bunk in the dark
so I wouldn't wake up Eli.

About halfway to the bathroom
to get a drink I bumped into someone.
It was Mr. Garbage on his way back.

We both yelled and jumped apart.
Mr. Garbage fell over a bag of cans.
I knocked into a tall pile of newspapers.
The piles of papers began toppling over
like stacks of dominos.
The whole room was crashing down on us.

"Help!" yelled Eli.
"We're having an earthquake!"

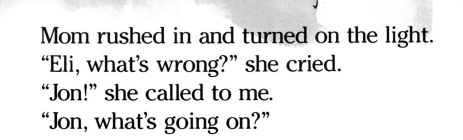

Mom rushed in and turned on the light.
"Eli, what's wrong?" she cried.
"Jon!" she called to me.
"Jon, what's going on?"

"We're having a garbage-quake!"
I called from under a pile of papers.
We spent the rest of the night
in sleeping bags on the floor
of Mom's room.

Roberta to the Rescue

I called Roberta the next morning.
"What's up?" she asked.
"We had a garbage-quake last night."
"You're joking," she said.
"Would you like to view the damage?"
I asked her.
"I'll be right over," said Roberta.
"Okay," I said.
"Put on your thinking cap.
We've got to find a way to stop Mr. Garbage."

Roberta was over in five minutes.
"Oh, brother," she said.
"This is not a neat room."
"Neat?" I yelled.
"This room is a disaster zone."

"Calm down," said Roberta.
"We need to make a plan."
"You have any ideas?" I asked.
"Yes," said Roberta.
"First, I don't think we should stop Eli
from saving the planet.

"That's the good part, and the bad part—"
"You don't need to tell me
about the bad part," I blurted out.
"You're looking at it."
"Hold on," said Roberta. "Here's my plan."
She pulled a paper from her pocket.
"Read," she said.
"I think this might work for Mr. Garbage."
I quickly read the free offer.
"Wow!" I said, "I could hug you, Roberta."

We rode our bikes to the Bean Sprout.
There was a sign in the window that read:

SAVE THE EARTH

PLANT A TREE

FREE SEEDLINGS

A lady in a tie-dyed dress
gave each of us a little tree.
"It just makes my heart feel good to see
kids helping save Mother Earth," she said.
We thanked her for the trees
and rode back to the house.
When we turned the corner to our block,
we got a huge surprise.

Every kid in the neighborhood was lined up
with wagons, strollers, wheelbarrows,
and shopping carts—
filling them up with junk from our room!

41

Mr. Garbage was standing on the steps
like a traffic cop.

Kids were bringing out paper,
bottles, cans, and plastic junk
like a steady stream of ants.
Mom was standing at the curb
with some other neighborhood moms.
We pulled up on our bikes.
"What's going on?" asked Roberta.

"The school asked us to deliver
Eli's recycling stuff today," said Mom.
"But how did all these kids get into
the act?" I asked.

Mom smiled and pointed to Eli.
"Mr. Garbage strikes again!" I said.
"Yes," said Mom.
"He rounded up every kid on the block.
Do you and Roberta want to help?"
"You bet!" we said together.

Mr. Garbage led the parade to school.
It was a day our neighborhood
will never forget.

It was the day I got back a junk-free room.
It was also the day Roberta and I
convinced Eli that planting trees
was a better way for him to save the earth.

But, knowing Eli, I'll take bets that
soon our block will look like a forest.
He started with the two little trees
Roberta and I gave him.
Last time we counted,
he had planted twenty already!